31 FEMALE
GHOSTS, MONSTERS, AND DEMONS
FROM AROUND THE WORLD

31 Female Ghosts, Monsters, and Demons From Around the World
(Illustrated Folklore Book 1)

Copyright © 2023 by Alex Kujawa

All rights reserved. No part of this book may be reproduced or utilized in any form or by any means, electronic or mechanical, including photocopying, recording, or by any information storage and retrieval system, without permission in writing from the authors, except in the case of brief excerpts or quotations embodied in critical articles and reviews.

Art & Graphic Design by Alex Kujawa
Written by Alex Kujawa & Scott Wheeler
Edited by Scott Wheeler

First Printing April 2018
Third Edition February 2023
ISBN 979-8-9866079-1-7

Wheejawa Publishing
PO Box 601
WOOD DALE, IL 60191-2094
www.AlexKujawa.com

For my husband Scott,
without whose *wordy words* help and encouragement this
book probably wouldn't have happened.

31 Female Ghosts, Monsters & Demons from Around the World

an illustrated folklore book

Alex Kujawa
with Scott Wheeler

Wheejawa Publishing
2023

From the artist:

What you are holding in your hand is something very special to me. It is a beginning of my most important art adventure. A labor of love, turning into a passion project, turning into a book series.

This book is a collection of drawings that I completed in the month of October 2017 as a part of the annual Inktober drawing event, in which artists from all over the world challenge themselves to post one new piece of art per day on social media. I started participating in this art event as early as 2014, but in 2017 I decided I was ready for a more intense project. At that time, I was interested in finding more about female folklore creatures from around the world, and thus my first book "31 Female Ghosts, Monsters, and Demons from Around the World" was born after a friend convinced me to publish the art project for others to enjoy. I myself enjoyed the research, art, and book design so much I have been making more of these since then.

By 2021 I had four different books completed, all on slightly different folklore subjects, yet all connected by my personal interest in Slavic mythology. This was also the year I decided it's best if I were to find a better printer to handle my beloved little books. During this whole process an unexpected opportunity arose to print my illustrations in full color, which is something I originally dreamed of for my books. I am absolutely delighted to revisit this artwork again.

So much love went into this book and I hope you'll enjoy it at least as much as I have. Thank you so much for picking it up and thank you for supporting my art adventures.

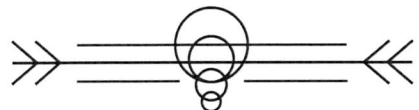

01. La Llorona *(Mexico)*
02. La Ciguapa *(Dominican Republic)*
03. Batibat *(Phillipines)*
04. Botan Dōrō *(Japan)*
05. Bożałość *(West Slavic Europe)*
06. Huldra *(Scandinavia)*
07. Sadako *(Japan)*
08. Południca *(Eastern Europe)*
09. Harpy *(Greek)*
10. Futakuchi-Onna *(Japan)*
11. Bloody Mary *(Britain)*
12. Zmora *(Slavic & Germanic Europe)*
13. Krasue *(South-East Asia)*
14. Sihuanaba *(Central America)*
15. La Lechuza *(Mexico)*
16. Soucouyant *(Caribbean)*
17. Licho *(Eastern Europe)*
18. Yuki-Onna *(Japan)*
19. Rusalka *(Eastern Europe)*
20. Pontianak *(Indonesia)*
21. Banshee *(Ireland)*
22. Strzyga *(Eastern Europe)*
23. Buschgroßmutter *(Germanic Europe)*
24. Kuchisake-Onna *(Japan)*
25. Nang Ta-Khian *(Thailand)*
26. Baba Yaga *(Eastern Europe)*
27. Mama D'Leau *(Caribbean)*
28. Dames Blanches *(France)*
29. Peri *(Persia)*
30. Headless Nun *(Canada)*
31. Manananggal *(Phillipines)*

Disclaimer:
This book is a work of art. It is not intended as a scientific manual or research source. Care was taken to ensure information is as complete and accurate as possible, but is in no way exhaustive or definitive.

La Llorona

LA LLORONA

LA LLORONA is a legendary ghost in Mexican folklore. She is the spirit of a beautiful woman named Maria who drowned her own children in an act of revenge against her husband after she learned he was cheating on her. She now wanders by rivers or lakes after dusk, weeping, and if she finds any lone children at night she will drown them while crying and begging for their forgiveness. It is said that those who hear her wailing are marked for death unless they immediately escape.

Other names:
The Weeping Woman

La Ciguapa

LA CIGUAPA are a type of succubus that inhabit the high mountains of the Dominican Republic. They live in caves and can be found in jungles, usually at night, as they are nocturnal creatures. They are beautiful naked women with golden brown or blue skin, backwards feet, and very long and lush hair that they often use to cover their nudity. They seduce men in order to kill them, eat them, or to keep them trapped forever. They can be hunted during the full moon with the help of a black and white polydactyl dog, but one must take care to not look La Ciguapa directly in the eye, which will cause the onlooker to become bewitched.

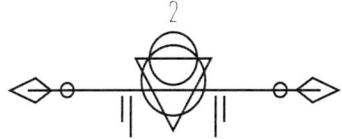

BATIBAT

BATIBAT

The BATIBAT is a demon found in the folklore of the Ilocano people of the Phillipines. Vengeful in nature, they were said to be the cause of bangungot, or unexplained nocturnal death. This comes about when a tree in which a Batibat resides is felled and used to build a home. If anyone sleeps too close to a beam or plank made from the wood of the Batibat's tree, it will take on the form of an old, tall, and very large fat woman, and sit on the sleeper's chest until they asphyxiate.

Other names:
Bangungot

Botan Dōrō

BOTAN DŌRŌ (Peony Lantern) is a popular kaidan (ghost story) from Japan involving a beautiful woman who lights her way with a peony lantern (sometimes carried by a servant), regularly visits a man at night, and always leaves before dawn. There are a few variations of the tale, but all involve an ongoing romantic relationship that is eventually found out by a servant, neighbor, or relative, who is suspicious of the woman and spies on the two of them at night. The man is seen to be in bed not with a beautiful woman, but with a skeleton, or otherwise with a decaying corpse. A priest or monk is summoned, who protects the house with ofuda (written paper talismans), preventing the woman from entering. Then after a while either the ofuda are removed or the man leaves the protection of the house to meet with the woman again, and ultimately his dead body is discovered embracing hers.

Other names
牡丹燈籠

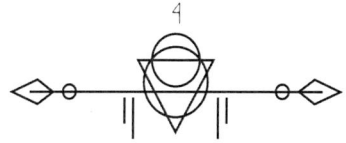

BOŽALOŠČ

BOŽALOŠČ is a messenger of death in Wendish (West Slavic) my-thology, in many ways similar to the banshee of Irish mythology. Her name means "God's lament" or "God's pity". She is described as a small woman dressed in white, with red eyes and long braided hair. She cries out of sight under the windows of people who are about to die.

Other names:
Božaloshtsh, Bozaloshtsh, Gottesklage

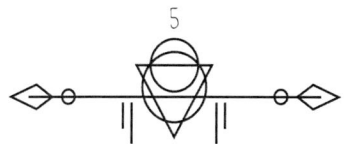

HULDRA

HULDRA is a seductive female forest creature found in Scandinavian folklore. She is described as a stunningly beautiful, sometimes naked woman with long hair; though from behind she has an animal's tail and her back is often hollow like an old tree trunk. Huldra like to lure men into the forest caves in order to harm them or keep them as slaves or lovers. They have also been known to actually marry local farm boys. However it is said that if a huldra is treated badly by her husband, she will remind him that she is far from weak by straightening out a horseshoe with her bare hands, sometimes while it is still glowing hot from the forge. The huld-rå being is a rå, which is a keeper or warden of a particular location or landform. As a whole, they are known as huldrefolk or huldufólk (hidden folk of the forest). However only the females tend to venture among humans, sometimes pretending to be simple farmer girls.

The male Hulder are very hideous, with grotesquely long noses.

Other names:
Skogsrå "forest spirit" or Tallemaja "pine tree Mary" (Swedish folklore), Ulda (Sámi folklore).
Her name suggests that she is originally the same being as the völva divine figure Huld and the German Holda.

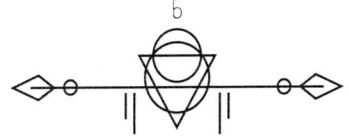

SADAKO

SADAKO's number is an urban legend from Japan that is connected to the Ring franchise created by Koji Suzuki. Some say that this urban legend was inspired by the novels or the movies, but others claim that it was the other way around. You can reach Sadako if you call a certain number, and those who are brave enough to try will hear her make a horrible inhuman shriek. Within seven days of the call something traumatizing will happen to you. The phone number is 090-4444-4444. In Japanese the number four (shi) sounds like the word for "death" (shi) and is considered to be an unlucky number in many East Asian cultures.

Other names:
貞子

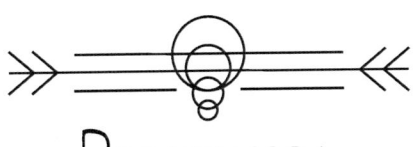

POŁUDNICA

POŁUDNICA is a mythical demon of the mid-day, common to the various Slavic countries of Eastern Europe. She is only seen on the hottest part of a summer's day and is the personification of a sun-stroke. She often takes the form of whirling dust clouds stalking her prey before assuming a human form. She may appear as an old hag, a beautiful woman, or a young girl, and she carries a scythe, sickle, or farmer's shears. Południca will stop people in the field to ask them difficult questions or engage them in conversation. If anyone fails to answer a question or tries to change the subject, she will cut off their head or strike them with illness or madness. Her tale has been useful in scaring children away from valuable crops.

Other names:
Południca in Polish, Полудница (Poludnitsa) in Serbian,
Bulgarian and Russian, Polednice in Czech,
Poludnica in Slovak, Připołdnica in Upper Sorbian,
Полозныча (Poloznicha) in Komi, Chirtel Ma in Yiddish,
and Noon Witch or Lady Midday in English.

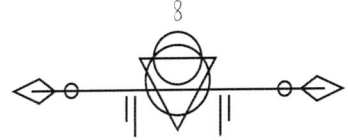

Harpy

A HARPY is a half-woman half-bird being from Greek mythology, the personification of storm wind. While usually depicted as beautiful in visual art, writers typically emphasised their hideousness. They were said to steal food from the hands of their victims, and one well-known story involving Harpies has them participating in the torture of Phineus by preventing him from eating by repeatedly robbing him of his food. Harpies were often named as the cause of sudden disappearances, that they had abducted an evildoer, who would then face torture on their way to Tartarus.

Other names:
ἅρπυια (Greek), harpȳia (Latin)

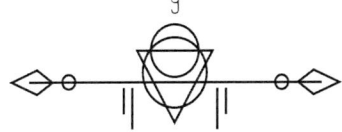

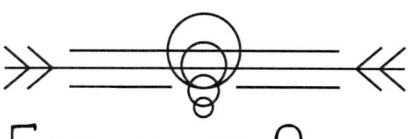

Futakuchi-Onna

FUTAKUCHI-ONNA (two-mouthed woman) is a yōkai (spirit or monster) in Japanese folklore. Otherwise human, the Futakuchi-Onna has a second mouth underneath her hair on the back of her head. Typically, the woman is never seen to eat food in the ordinary way, and instead eats in secret using her second mouth, which is insatiable. Her hair comes alive and helps grasp and bring food into the disgusting, always-hungry mouth. The nature of this monster is more of a supernatural curse that affects the woman host as a result of hunger brought on by eating very little for a long time, sometimes as the result of a stingy husband refusing to feed her.

Other names:
二口女

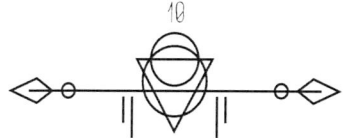

Bloody Mary

BLOODY MARY is a British folklore legend consisting of a ghost, phantom, or spirit conjured to reveal the future. She is said to appear in a mirror when her name is called three times. This is done by repeatedly chanting her name in a mirror placed in a dimly-lit or candle-lit room. The Bloody Mary apparition appears as a corpse, a witch, or a ghost. She can be friendly or evil, and is sometimes "seen" covered in blood. The lore surrounding the ritual states that participants may endure the apparition screaming at them, cursing them, strangling them, stealing their soul, drinking their blood, or scratching their eyes out. Pictured here holding the alcoholic drink of the same name, which is otherwise unrelated to the legend.

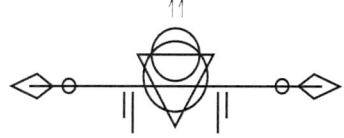

ZMORA

ZMORA is an evil spirit in Slavic and Germanic folklore that rides on people's chests while they sleep, causing nightmares. She is often depicted as a skinny, tall woman with inhumanly long legs and a translucent body. She is a shapeshifter, and can disguise herself as a moth, mouse, or other small animal, but can also turn into small objects such as a needle. She enters people's houses through keyholes. She feeds on the blood or life force of sleeping humans, bringing on bad dreams and sleep paralysis. She has also been known to entangle (or sometimes braid) the hair of sleeping people, or that of animals, or in some cases tree branches. Zmora were also believed to "ride" horses, which left the horses exhausted and covered in sweat by the morning.

Other names:
Mare (English and Old Dutch), Mære (Old English),
Mara (in Old High German, Old Norse, and
Old Church Slavic), Nocna Zmora (Polish)

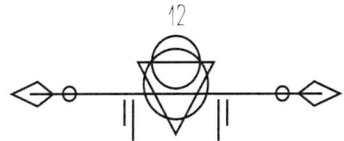

KRASUE

KRASUE

The KRASUE is a type of nocturnal vampiric spirit that appears in South-East Asian folklore. Its origins and behavior vary by region, but it always has the form of the floating head of a beautiful young woman, with disembodied organs hanging below it. It is sometimes depicted with sharp vampire-like fangs, and/or a long proboscis-like tongue, both of which are used for sucking blood. It is drawn to blood, and is said to prey upon pregnant women in particular, and also on carrion. Defenses usually involve placing spiked objects or thorny plants around an area, as these will snag the hanging organs of the Krasue.

Other names:
Krasue (Thai: กระสือ, /krà.sɯ̌ː/), Ahp in Cambodia,
Kasu (Lao: ກະສື, /ka.sɯ̌ː/) in Laos;
Penanggalan or Hantu Penanggal in Malaysia;
Leyak, Palasik, Selaq Metem, Kuyang, Poppo,
and Parakang in Indonesia
(there's probably more, this one really gets around)

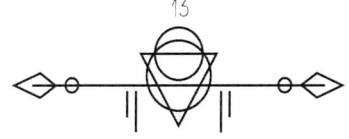

Sihuanaba

Sihuanaba

SIHUANABA is a Central American spirit that lures men, and takes form in variations on a theme, depending on who glimpses it. To unfaithful men it will appear as a beautiful young woman. To faithful men it will appear as the man's spouse or lover. To young boys it will appear as their mother. It typically appears seen only from behind, naked or clad in sheer and flimsy clothing, washing or combing its hair. When its target gets close it will reveal its face to be either that of a horse, or a skull, which either kills the man of fright or drives him insane. The man may simply wander to his doom in search of the Sihuanaba, a sort of Siren of the desert.

Other names:
La Siguanaba, Cihuanaba, Sihuanaba, Ciguanaba, Ciguapa, Cigua, or Cegua

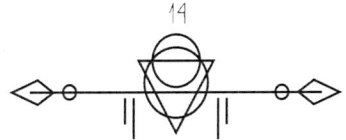

La Lechuza

La Lechuza

LA LECHUZA (literally "owl" or "barn owl") is a creature in Hispanic folklore in Texas and Mexico, similar to the Harpy of Greek mythology. La Lechuza is a human-sized bird with the face of a woman, and also like the Harpy it has a connection with storms and the ability to cause them. Unlike the Harpy, La Lechuza is a shape-shifter, being either a witch who changes form at night to fly around looking for prey, or the returned vengeful spirit of such a woman. It is said to perch out of sight and mimic the sound of a crying baby in order to lure human prey.

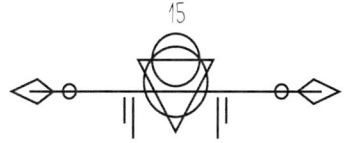

SOUCOUYANT

SOUCOUYANT is a type of blood sucking hag in Caribbean folklore. The Soucouyant practices black magic. She is a shapeshifter who appears as a reclusive old woman by day. By night, she strips off her wrinkled skin and puts it in a mortar. In her true form as a fireball, she flies across the dark sky in search of a victim. The Soucouyant can enter the home of her victim through any sized hole like cracks, crevices, and keyholes. Soucouyants suck people's blood from their arms, legs, and soft parts while they sleep, leaving blue-black marks on the body in the morning. If the Soucouyant draws too much blood, it is believed that the victim will either die, become a Soucouyant themselves, or perish entirely, leaving the Soucouyant to assume their skin.

Other names:
Soucriant (in Dominican,
St. Lucian, Trinidadian, Guadeloupean folklore),
Lougarou (in Haiti, Louisiana, and Grenada),
Ole-Higue or Ole Haig (in Guyana and Jamaica),
and Asema (Suriname)

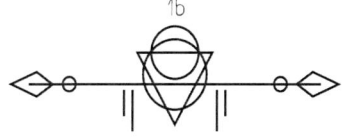

Licho nie śpi Licho wie
ma Licho więto Licho do licha
pal gdzieś go Licho nie sre Licho
Licho do Licha Licho nie
Licho Licho Śni

Licho

LICHO is an embodiment of evil fate and misfortune in Slavic mythology. It is a demon usually depicted as either an old, ugly, skinny woman with one eye, or as a small shaggy wide-eyed goblin of the forest. Licho is most powerful in the old woman form. She is attracted to happy households and communities, which she seeks to destroy. She causes mischief by misplacing or destroying people's belongings, damaging property, causing fires, tormenting pets or farm animals, and by bringing all kinds of sickness to crops, animals, or people. Licho sometimes focuses on one individual, usually a kind and good person, trying to corrupt them. She will haunt them by whispering all kinds of lies, bad thoughts, and ideas in to their ear, trying to bring them astray and often causing madness. Licho never sleeps, and there is no proven way of protecting yourself against it or fighting it off. If you are haunted by Licho you simply have to wait for it to get tired of you and leave.

Other names:
Licho (Polish), Лихо (Russian), ліха (Belarusian),
Likho or Liho (English)

Yuki-Onna

YUKI-ONNA (snow woman) is a Japanese yokai (spirit) that takes the form of a beautiful woman, usually with long black hair, pale skin, and blue lips. There are a variety of regional stories and variations involving Yuki-Onna as a sort of stock character, but all involve her connection with snow and the cold. She will typically be encountered in a snowstorm, sometimes nude, and sometimes holding a young child. A parent searching for their own lost child may come across her in this form, and she will offer them the child she is carrying, which results in them being frozen solid on the spot. The Yuki-Onna may appear at a house during a snowstorm, as though seeking shelter, and will then either disappear under mysterious circumstances (such as melting in the bath) or summon an especially strong wind from the snowstorm to destroy the home.

Other names:
雪女

RUSALKA

RUSALKA is a water spirit in Slavic folklore. Sometimes translated as "Mermaid" though they are in fact entirely different entities. Historically held to be benevolent spirits who brought moisture to the land during growing season, the last few centuries have seen the rise of more sinister stories. A Rusalka will appear as an extremely beautiful woman, and lure men to the water where shen then drowns them, sometimes while being tickled by the Rusalka as she laughs. Some traditions state that the Rusalka cannot entirely leave the water, and must at least keep their feet submerged, while other tales have them fully capable of mobility beyond the water. Their activity is often viewed as seasonal, being more active during different times of the year, with regional variation.

Other names:
Rusałka (Polish), Русáлка (Russian)

Pontianak

PONTIANAK is a vampiric female spirit appearing primarily in Indonesian and Malaysian folklore, with additional variations in other South-East Asian countries. It is said to reside in banana trees and comes out to find prey at the full moon. It makes a high-pitched cry like that of a baby, and emits a scent that is at first floral but followed by the stench of decay. It will use its sharp fingernails to rip open the stomach of its victims in order to consume their internal organs. It can be attracted by the smell of its victims' laundry, leading superstitious people to refuse to dry laundry by hanging it outside. A defense against the Pontianak is to drive a nail in to the base of its neck, which will cause it to become simply a beautiful woman who will "make a good wife" so long as the nail remains in place.

Other names:
Boentianak (Dutch-Indonesian), فونتيانق (Jawi),
Matianak, Kuntilanak, Kunti (Indonesian variations)

BANSHEE

BANSHEE

BANSHEE (woman of the fairy mound) is an Irish female spirit, known primarily for her shrieking or keening. Connected to the Gaelic tradition of keening to mourn the dead, the Banshee is said to do this either to herald the death of a recently deceased family member, or to predict that someone is soon to die. A Banshee can appear as either beautiful or ugly, wearing green or red, and has red or blonde hair that shimmers like fire. Banhees are not themselves malevolent, but are rather seen as an ill omen. Banshees are particularly Irish, and are commonly believed to only perform their keening for members of pure Irish families.

Other names:
bean sí, ban síde

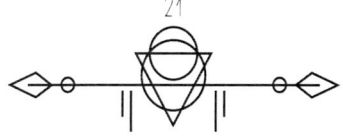

STRZYGA

Strzyga

STRZYGA is a type of vampiric demon from Slavic demononlogy. Sometimes a child will be born with two hearts, two souls, and two rows of teeth, and this child will grow in to a Strzyga. Such babies, if stillborn, must be buried face down to prevent them from coming back as a Strzyga. If they do come back they will grow long claws and sharp teeth, and they will feed on the blood and organs of animals, or preferably that of humans. They are disproportionately strong for their size, and are believed to be able to take the form of an owl to fly in search of prey. Methods for killing a Strzyga include burning their bodies while they sleep, and decapitation followed by burying their head away from their body. They can also be dealt with by spending a night in their tomb sleeping face-down, which may have the effect of curing them. The masculine form of the same is Strzygon. From Latin "Strix" meaning "Owl" and referring to a winged being of ill omen, and ultimately from the same root as "Strigoi" (Romanian) which is the predecessor of the modern vampire as popularized by Bram Stoker.

Other names:
Strzyg or Strzygoń (male version), Stryha (Belarusian: Стрыга)

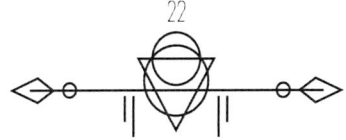

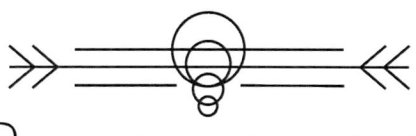

Buschgrossmutter

BUSCHGROßMUTTER, also known as "Shrub Granny", is a legendary creature from Germanic folklore. She is a forest spirit living in the deepest of woods, and shows herself to humans only once every hundred years. Her appearance is described as being small, hunched, wrinkly, and ugly. Her feet are overgrown with moss, and her hair is long, white, cold as ice, lousy, and very tangled. She will ask people to comb her hair, and rewards those who do with yellow leaves which, if kept and treasured, will turn in to actual gold. She punishes those who sneer at her by breathing on them, which brings sickness and a rash.

Other names:

Buschgrossmutter (older orthography), Pusch-Grohla ("shrub granny") or Buschweibchen ("shrub woman", with Weibchen being the diminutive of Weib, "woman")

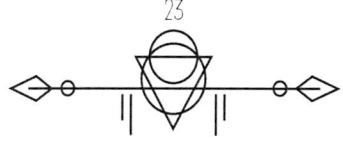

KUCHISAKE-ONNA

KUCHISAKE-ONNA

KUCHISAKE-ONNA (slit-mouthed woman) is a Japanese onryō (vengeful spirit) that has appeared in Japanese folklore and urban myth since as early as the Edo period (1603-1868). Her mouth is slit open at each side, giving her a horrifying visage. According to legend, after discovering she had been having an affair with another man, her mouth was cut open by her husband, who asked "who will find you pretty now?" She will appear to potential victims with her mouth covered by a fan, scarf, or surgical mask, and will ask them "Am I pretty?" which results in a no-win scenario. Answering that she is pretty will cause her to slash your mouth open the same way. Answering that she is not pretty will result in her stalking you and killing you that night. The defense against her is to confuse her, either with an non-commital response (saying she is "so-so" or "average"), asking her a question like if she thinks you are pretty, or by throwing fruit or candy at her which will distract her as you run away.

Other names:
口裂け女

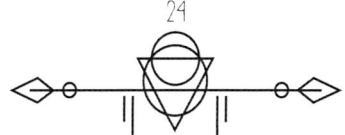

NANG TA-KHIAN

NANG TA-KHIAN (lady of the ta-khian tree) is a female spirit in Thai folklore who gets her name from haunting the ta-khian tree. It is said that she will also haunt a house made from the wood of a ta-khian tree, leading to these trees being very rarely used for lumber. She is not considered a malicious spirit, and will only harm immoral or bad people who come too close to her haunt. For this reason, one of the few places where ta-khian wood is used as a building material is in buddhist monasteries, as the monks are considered virtuous enough to have nothing to fear from the tree spirits. Still, the trees are only felled for this purpose after a ceremony is performed to ask the spirit's permission. Older ta-khian trees are often wrapped with coloured cloth by buddhist monks to protect the spirits' abode from logging, and to protect humans from the spirits' wrath.

Other names:
นางตะเคียน (Thai)

Baba Yaga

BABA YAGA is a supernatural witch appearing in a variety of stories in all Slavic countries. She is usually depicted as being deformed or ugly, and she may fly around in a mortar and wield a pestle as a weapon, or otherwise inhabit a forest hut propped up on chicken legs or a single chicken leg. Not necessarily malevolent, the nature and role of Baba Yaga varies greatly from tale to tale, and the character may even appear as a trio of sisters all bearing the same name. Her nature is as varied as the stories in which she appears, and though it is difficult to lay an unambigious single definition or nature upon her, Baba Yaga is an archetype in Slavic folklore.

Other names:
Баба-яга (Russian), Баба Яга (Bulgarian), Baba Jaga (Polish)

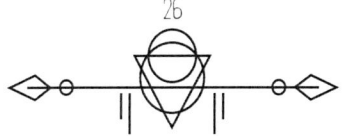

Mama D'Leau

MAMA DLEAU (mother of the water) is a spirit that appears in several forms in Caribbean folklore, particularly among African diaspora, and has several related entities in West African culture. She will appear often sitting on a rock by a body of water, a beautiful woman with long hair either black or golden. She is a healer and protector of nature, especially river animals. If provoked, she will transform in to a serpent-like beast with a forked tongue, armour of scales, and snakes for hair.

Other names:
Mama Dlo, Mama Glo

Dames Blanches

DAMES BLANCHES (white ladies) are female spirits in French folklore. They are said to inhabit choke points along travel routes, such as bridges or natural features of the land, where they would impede passers-by. Unlike Trolls lurking under bridges, the toll demanded by one of les Dames Blanches was usually to dance with her. If a traveller dances with her, she will be pleasant and allow them to pass, vanishing soon after. If refused, she would throw the traveller off the path, or have her animal followers torment them.

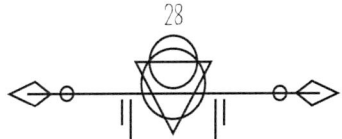

Peri

PERI

PERI is a being originating in Persian mythology; beautiful, winged, and pixie-like, somewhat similar to an angel, though with a more ambiguous nature. Early depictions portrayed Peri as malevolent demonic beings, but later on they also appeared as benevolent. An early Peri tale involves them being fallen good spirits who were denied access to paradise until they had atoned for some misdeed. Peri were also incorporated in to Islamic lore, wherein they were created by God and are viewed as a good variant of Jinn.

Other names:
Persian: پری pari, plural پریان pariān

Headless Nun

The HEADLESS NUN is a Canadian ghost tale of a French nun known as Sister Marie or Sister Marie Innocue ("unknown") who was beheaded in the 1700's in French Fort Cove (modern day Northumberland County, New Brunswick). Details leading up to her beheading vary by source, but her head was ultimately separated from her body and never recovered, while her body was returned to France, leading to her decapitated spirit continuing to haunt the area of her death in search of her head. Her spectre is said to approach people at night, asking them to find her head; or otherwise to appear bearing her own head in her arms, requesting that it be returned to be buried with her body.

Other names:
bonne sœur sans tête (French)

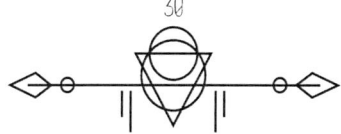

MANANANGGAL

MANANANGGAL is a mythical monster from the Philippines. Its name comes from Tagalog and translates to "one who separates itself". Usually depicted as female and hideously ugly. Its most notable feature is that it can separate its upper body from its lower, approximately at the waist, and sprout wings, which it does at night in order to fly around in search of prey. It will suck blood and also prey upon pregnant women, similar to the Krasue of other South-East Asian folklore. While the upper body flies around, its lower body remains in place on the ground and vulnerable, and it can be defeated by spreading salt or garlic on the severed portion of the lower body, which will prevent the Manananggal from being able to reconnect itself before sunrise, causing it to be destroyed. It shares many attributes with, and is partially inspired by, European tales of vampires.

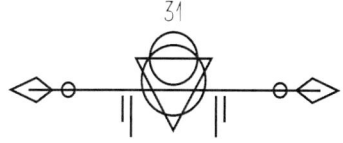

Alex Kujawa is a graphic artist and illustrator based in the Chicago area, where she lives with her husband and cats. She was born in Poland and moved to the United States in her teens, where she attended Harper College and Judson University. Her personal style has evolved as a blending of creepy and beautiful, being inspired by the art nouveau movement, as well as horror and dark fantasy. She usually works in ink with pen and marker, and occasionally adds digital color. She has worked on a wide variety of art projects, including illustrations for "WITCH: Fated Souls" tabletop RPG by Angry Hamster Publishing, and the "Ice Zombies" comic book by Waterfoot Comics. She began her series of illustrated folklore books in 2017, but has been illustrating folklore creatures for far longer. To see more of Alex's art, follow her on social media through AlexKujawa.com

WHEEJAWA PUBLISHING

Copyright ©2023 by Alex Kujawa
Illustrated by Alex Kujawa
Written by Alex Kujawa and Scott Wheeler

www.AlexKujawa.com

OTHER BOOKS IN THIS SERIES:

🐝 31 SLAVIC BEINGS OF MYTH & MAGIC:
Probably the most intensively researched book in the series, choosing the theme of Slavic Beings of Myth and Magic as a means for the author to learn more about her Slavic pagan heritage. This book contains 31 illustrations and background information on the particular being, including deities, spirits, and creatures.
ISBN 979-8-9866079-3-1

💀 31 GHOST STORIES:
Ranging from famous to more obscure and even including a personal story, this book contains 31 illustrations and background information on each particular ghost. All ghost stories are tied to places and a majority of the ghosts are named, and circumstances of their deaths explained.
ISBN 979-8-9866079-2-4

🐈 31 SUPERNATURAL FELINES:
The fourth in the illustrated folklore series, this book dives in to various world mythologies and folklore, introducing 31 of the most fascinating feline creatures of supernatural origin, as chosen by the artist, who tends to favor Slavic mythology.
ISBN 979-8-9866079-4-8